From the Fly me to the Moon Bubba Series

Colour your Moon with Bubba

Special thanks to:
Laurie Tissington, Frida Abaroa, Doris Schulz
Sarah 'Shiro' Parr, Yanet Zamudio Castro
Omar Lara Cadó, Gabriela Lopez Vidal, Omar Lara Cadó
Dustin Cromarty, Miriam Hick

Cookingwith Monkey ©
Productions Corporation

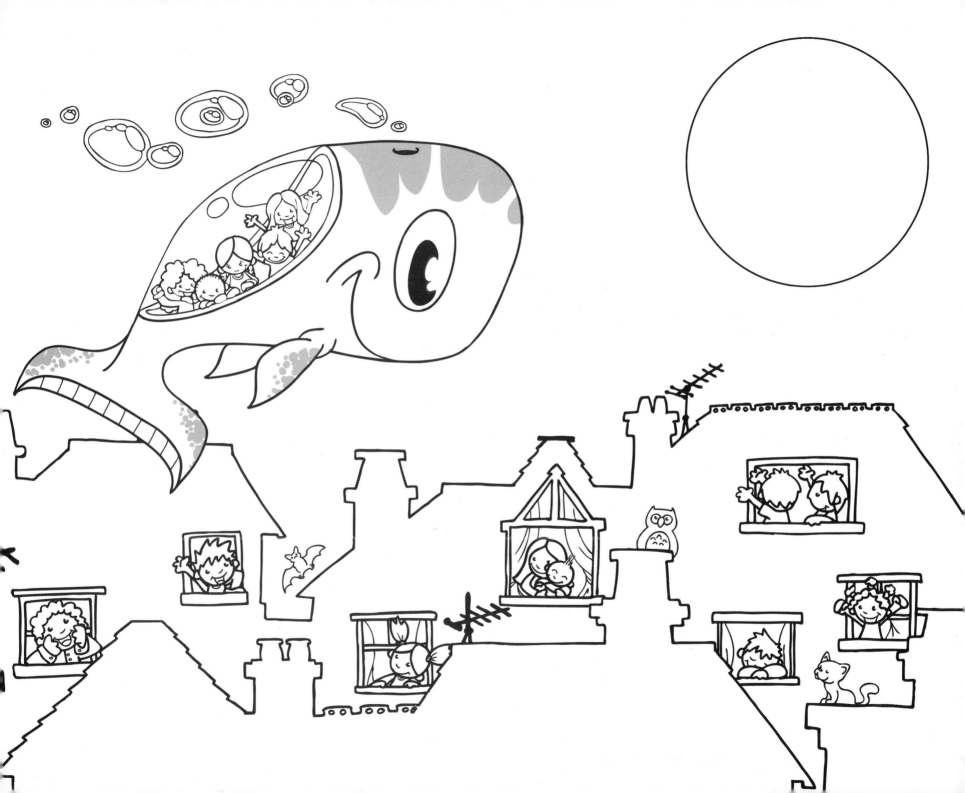

**Connect the dots
From one to two,**

**Then three to four,
Keep on going more
And more**

**And you'll discover
Who they're for.**

**Storyflowers is what
They pick,**

**These two little elves
Are very quick!**

**To solve this game,
Connect the numbers.**

**Go up and up 'till you
Can no longer.**

**A little monkey then
You'll discover;**

**She's so much fun,
You're gonna love her!**

This little guy was so sad,

'Cause he didn't know
What he had.

Rockets Up came
To his rescue

And all sadness from
Him withdrew.

Connect the dots and
See what is true.

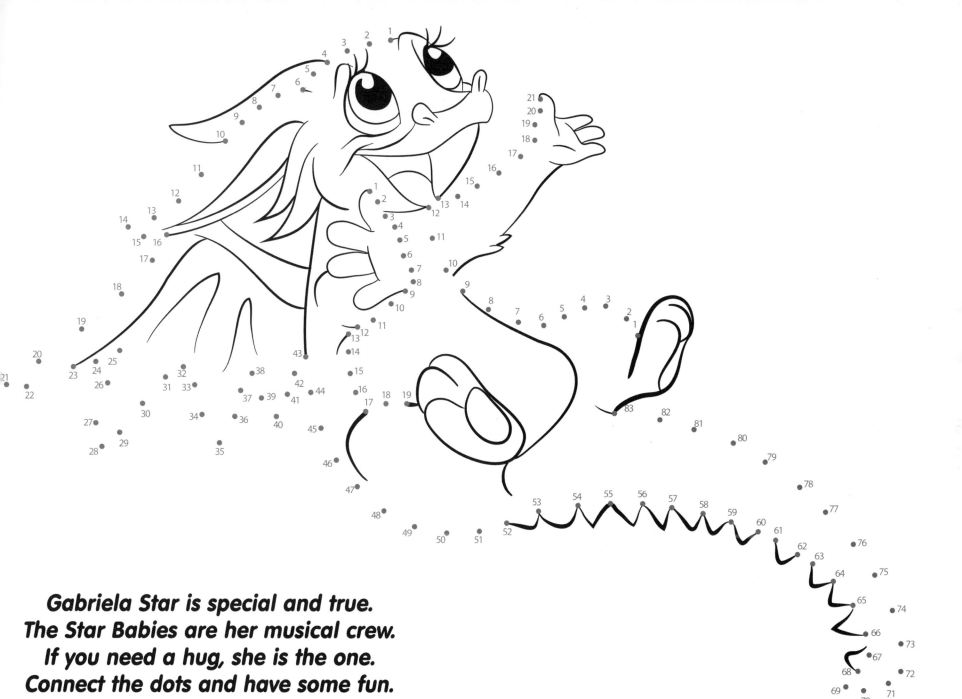

Gabriela Star is special and true.
The Star Babies are her musical crew.
If you need a hug, she is the one.
Connect the dots and have some fun.

Connect the dots indeed,
And do it with speed,

For this character loves action,
Precision and traction.

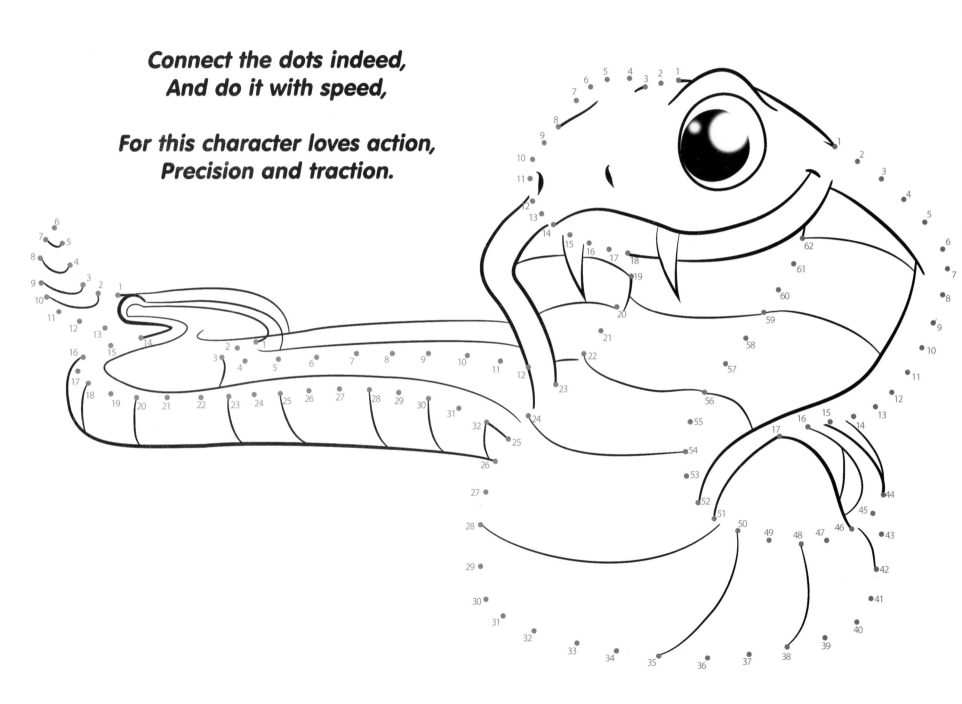

I am a kid,
Just like you.

Shall we colour
Bubba blue?

I Spy Game!

Find **4** Wee Monkeys

Find **6** Moonsicles

Find **6** Stars

I Spy Game!

Find **4** Wee Monkeys

Find **4** Kazaam Wham Wow